My
Spooky
Sister

Other titles by Sandra Glover

My Spooky Sister

SANDRA GLOVER

Andersen Press · London

First published in 2004 by
Andersen Press Limited,
20 Vauxhall Bridge Road, London SW1V 2SA
www.andersenpress.co.uk

British Library Cataloguing in Publication Data available
ISBN 1 84270 280 7

Typeset by FiSH Books, London WC1
Printed and bound in Great Britain by Mackays of Chatham Ltd.,
Chatham, Kent

Chapter 1

Maybe it's not a very nice thing to say but my sister is weird. Though I didn't realise quite how weird until about a year ago, when she helped to solve a murder case. Not bad for someone who was only eight years old at the time!

But it was whose murder she helped to solve and how she did it which make the case...and my sister...seem a bit spooky.

Right from the start, my sister was strange. I

was only three when she was born, so I guess I don't remember much of it first hand. It's mainly based on stuff my parents have told me.

We knew the baby was going to be a girl because Mum had one of those tests. But Mum says I wasn't very interested in a baby of any sort, girl or boy. I asked whether we could just have a kitten instead.

So my parents tried to get me more involved. Choosing baby clothes, baby toys, baby names.

Maybe asking me to help choose a name was a bit of a mistake. My first choice was Paddington.

'Paddington's a lovely name for a bear, Tom,' Mum said. 'But I'm not sure it's right for a little girl.'

So I guess that ruled out 'Pooh' as well.

My other suggestions such as 'Bambi' or 'Gloop' weren't great successes either.

'Don't you know any nice girls' names, Tom?' Mum pleaded.

We settled on Jessica. Mum liked it. Dad liked it. And I came round to it once Dad had pointed out that we could shorten it to 'Jess' like Postman Pat's cat.

Then my sister was born and the first odd thing happened. Mum took one look at her and said:

'She doesn't look like a Jessica.'

'Er, doesn't she?' said Dad. 'What does she look like then?'

'Alice,' said Mum. 'She looks like an Alice. I want to call her Alice.'

Not that it's unusual for people to change their minds about a baby's name. And I don't suppose any of us would have given it a second thought, if it hadn't been for what happened later.

Anyway, Alice Jessica she became. Or Ally, as she prefers to be called these days.

There are two other things I ought to tell you about Alice when she was a baby. Firstly, she cried a lot. Well, OK, all babies cry. But Alice cried all the time. Day and night. Not just when she was hungry, bored or tired. But all the time. Like she was really, really miserable.

Mum and Dad were pretty miserable too. They were shattered. And Mum was always at the doctor's asking him to look at Alice. Mum was sure there must be something seriously wrong. Like Alice must be in pain or something. But the doctor never found anything.

'She's a beautiful baby, Mrs Kingsley,' he'd say. 'And perfectly healthy. So stop worrying! Babies can pick up feelings of anxiety, you know. You're probably passing your worries on to her.'

'Oh, so it's my fault now, is it?' Mum would snap, utterly exhausted as Alice howled and bawled in her arms.

The second thing I want to tell you involves photographs. Me and Alice looked very similar when we were babies. Same size. Same shape. Scattered wisps of blond hair falling in exactly the same places. Greyish-green eyes.

Put our baby pics side by side and you can barely tell us apart. Except for the expressions on our faces. I'm always beaming. Grinning like a mad baboon.

But Alice always has a frown on her face. Her little forehead's all screwed up and wrinkly. Eyes down. Thumb in mouth. She's like that on all the photographs. Every single one. I've never seen such a worried-looking baby.

Luckily, by the time she was six months old, Alice had calmed down a touch. She was still a bit of a misery guts but she didn't cry quite so much. And, when she did, you could usually shut her up by dangling a toy in front of her or pulling a silly face.

And it wasn't all bad news with Alice. She's always been very clever. Very advanced for her age. Everybody said so. For a start, Alice never bothered with crawling. She just pulled herself up one day and off she went. Walking across the room with barely a wobble.

She started talking early too. And that's when the real problems began.

Chapter 2

My first word was 'dadda'. Not very original but then I'm a fairly ordinary sort of kid. My first full sentence was 'Me done wee wee'. Lousy grammar and, as there was a puddle already spreading across the floor, I needn't have bothered mentioning it at all. The evidence spoke for itself.

Compare that with Alice. Her first word was 'footsteps'. She just came out and said it one day. Mum thought she must have misheard. But no, Alice said it again. 'Footsteps.' Think about it. It's not an easy word for a tiny kid to say but Alice said it so clearly that Mum stopped. Listened. Expected to hear the crunch of the postman coming up the path. But there was nothing.

After a while we got used to Alice coming out with strange words. Sort of grown-up words. Dad said she was probably just a very good listener. Picking words up from TV or when she was out and about. Repeating them at home days later.

I wish Mum and Dad could remember more of the words she said back then. Because I've got a feeling they could be important. Three early words of Alice's that I remember are all names. Harry, Katy and Mark. And they're definitely important, as you'll see later.

Anyway, every time Alice played, those were the names she used. All her dolls and teddies were called either Harry, Katy or Mark.

As for Alice's first sentences. Well, some of those were real shockers.

'I want to go home.'

I'm not sure whether that was the first. But it was certainly one of the first and as she was sitting on Dad's knee on the settee in our lounge at the time, it seemed a bit odd. Not least because it was a proper sentence.

Just as Alice never bothered with crawling, she didn't bother much with baby talk either. Her early sentences might have been short but they were perfectly formed.

'I'm not Alice,' was one of her others. 'I'm Alison.'

She got into quite a strop when we carried on calling her Alice.

'I've told you!' she'd scream out in shops. 'I'm not Alice. I'm Alison. Alison Smith. And I don't want to live with you. I want to go home.'

It was a bit upsetting when my sister kept saying she didn't want to live with us. And bewildered passers-by would stare at us, like we were kidnapping her or something. One old lady actually phoned the police one day. Dad had gone to collect Alice from playgroup. He made the mistake of saying:

'That's a lovely painting, Alice,' as he was about to get her into the car.

'I'm not Alice,' she screamed, throwing herself to the floor. 'You're not my dad. I'm not going with you.'

Poor Dad had just picked up the screaming Alice, when the police arrived. Boy, was Dad embarrassed. Showing his driving licence, by way of identification, wasn't enough. Not with Alice still yelling that it wasn't her name and he wasn't her dad.

She was Alison Smith, not Alice Kingsley, she claimed. She was very convincing for a three-year-old and it was clear the policemen believed her. So in the end Dad had to get the playgroup leader out to say who he was.

After that, we decided on Ally. Telling my sister that it was short for both Alice and Alison. But the battle over the name was actually the least of our problems where my sister was concerned.

Bedtimes were the worst. I don't want to boast or anything but I've always been a really good sort of kid.

'Tom's no trouble,' is what people usually say about me.

Not exactly the best compliment in the world, but true enough. I'm no genius. I'm not even very bright. But I'm fairly laid back. Fairly easy going. And no trouble.

Quick bath, a splash around with my boat and my plastic frog, warm drink, one story and that was it. I was off to sleep. Usually spark out before the story was even finished.

Not so with my sister. Most nights she'd have to be carried upstairs sobbing and kicking. She'd demand story after story. She'd want to go to the loo. Go downstairs for another drink. Anything to put off the moment when she had to go to sleep.

And who could blame her? Sleep, for Ally, wasn't the peaceful sort of experience it was for me. She'd toss, turn, scream. Cry out. And her cries were always the same. Someone was going to hurt her. Hurt the children.

'Who's going to hurt you?' Mum would ask. 'Which children?'

Ally could never say. She'd stare around her

bedroom, miserable and confused. As though she didn't even know where she was.

Every single night she woke us up. But it wasn't only the nightmares that were freaky. It was the things Ally was saying during the day, when she was wide awake.

By the time Ally was four, she was talking at least as well as me. And I was seven! But whereas I talked about ordinary things like school, friends and TV programmes, Ally seemed to live in a complete fantasy world. Always talking about her 'other family'.

'My other mummy didn't make me eat carrots,' she'd say.

Or,

'I'd like another rabbit. We used to have a rabbit. It was black and fluffy. But I didn't have a brother then.'

Our doctor said not to worry. That Ally was a bright child. An imaginative child. That her ramblings were just a clever way of trying to get what she wanted. Did that mean she'd rather have a black, fluffy bunny than a big brother?

The doctor also said that the 'other family'

were imaginary friends. That they'd go away once Ally started school and had more things to distract her.

He was right too. Once Ally started full-time school, she stopped talking about the 'other family' so much but she still had the nightmares and that's how the accident happened.

Chapter 3

Basically the nightmares were getting worse. Much worse. One night we heard a scream and before anyone could reach her, Ally was out of bed, running towards the stairs. She tripped, fell the full length of them. There were no broken bones or anything but she knocked herself unconscious.

She'd started to come round before the ambulance arrived but it was scary. Really scary. Poor Ally was in hospital for over a week. And it wasn't easy for Mum and Dad either. Not least because of all the forms they had to fill in. All the questions they had to answer.

'It's like they think we pushed her or something!' Mum said.

'No they don't,' said Dad. 'They're just doing the standard checks. They have to be careful, don't they?'

He didn't sound very convinced. And Ally wasn't really helping. Not when she'd wake up, on the ward, screaming:

'He mustn't hurt them! Don't let him hurt the children.'

'Don't let who hurt them, darling?' a nurse would say.

'The man,' Ally would sob. 'The bad man.'

When Mum told the hospital doctors that Ally had nightmares every single night, they were worried. They told Mum to put a baby gate back at the top of the stairs and booked Ally an appointment with a child psychologist.

Unfortunately there was a long waiting list. Mum wasn't prepared to wait and paid to see someone privately. But I guess she didn't make a very good choice of doctor because she was in a foul mood when she got home.

'Psychologist!' I heard Mum hiss at Dad, that night. 'Psychopath more likely. Loony. Headcase. Nuttier than most of his patients, I reckon. Do you know what he told me? Do you know what he said?'

'Er, no,' said Dad. 'I wasn't there, remember? I won't know until you tell me.'

'Reincarnation,' Mum said. 'The idiot man started droning on about reincarnation.'

I didn't know what that meant, so I hovered outside the kitchen door, hoping to find out. I wasn't disappointed.

'He reckons we've all lived before,' Mum said. 'That we might have lived lots of different lives. Can you believe that? I mean he's a doctor! You'd think he'd have more sense! Anyway he said that Ally shows all the classic signs of reincarnation. Of remembering a past life, before she was born into this one!'

'Like what?' asked Dad. 'What signs?'

'Apparently,' said Mum, 'kids who remember

15

past lives are often very bright, like Ally. But sort of troubled too. Cry a lot as babies. Tend to have a lot of nightmares which are when most of the past memories come out.'

'Memories of a past life,' said Dad, thoughtfully. 'Reincarnation. You know I saw a TV programme about that once. There were some pretty convincing cases. So I suppose it's possible.'

'No, Bill, it's not possible,' my mum said. 'It's mumbo-jumbo. Rot. Rubbish. Ridiculous.'

Well, it sounded fairly stupid to me. But sort of interesting too. So I stuck my head round the door.

'So if everyone's had past lives,' I said. 'If we've all lived before . . . how come we don't all remember? How come it's just Ally?'

'Exactly!' said my mother.

'Well actually,' said Dad, a bit sheepishly. 'People who believe in reincarnation DO have an explanation for that.'

'I bet they do!' Mum sneered.

'And it's not just Ally,' Dad went on. 'Hundreds of people, maybe even thousands claim to remember past lives.'

'I know,' said Mum. 'The psychologist told me. Most of us don't remember our past lives but lots of people do. The ones who ... '

She stopped. Looked at me.

'I'm not sure we ought to be discussing this in front of Tom.'

'Mum!' I said. 'I'm nearly nine. I'm not a baby.'

'It's all rubbish anyway,' said Mum. 'But what the psychologist said is that the ones who remember usually haven't died peacefully. They've met sudden or violent ends in their last life.'

'Wow!' I said. 'You mean like Ally might have died in a car crash or an explosion or been shot or something?'

'See!' said Mum. 'See what we're filling his head with! Now don't you dare mention this in front of Ally, Tom.'

'But she must have heard the doctor, the psychologist,' I pointed out. 'You know what she's like for picking things up.'

'Fortunately,' said Mum, 'Ally was in the play area, at the time. With one of the nurses. She didn't hear any of it.'

'And I don't suppose the psychologist had any suggestions, did he?' said Dad. 'I mean practical suggestions about what we can do about Ally's nightmares, or anything?'

'He said they'll probably pass, in time. As people get older, real memories of this life replace the old ones from the past life,' Mum explained. 'Very few adults remember past lives. It only ever comes out in adults if they're hypnotised or something.'

'So does he want to see Ally again?' Dad asked.

'Are you mad?' said Mum, by way of an answer. 'I'm not paying good money to have some crazy witch doctor filling Ally's head with rubbish. No way! We'll handle this ourselves.'

'You know what I reckon,' said Dad. 'I reckon we all need a holiday. A nice long holiday. I could take a couple of weeks in summer. Get away for a bit.'

Quite an offer from Dad. He's a self-employed electrician. Bit of a workaholic. Hardly ever takes so much as a day off, let alone a two-week holiday.

'Where do you fancy?' he asked.

'Disneyland,' I said, determined to make the most of the opportunity.

'Greece,' said Mum.

'Scarborough,' said Ally, when we asked her.

'Scarborough?' said Dad. 'Why Scarborough?'

'I like Scarborough,' said Ally.

'How do you know?' I said. 'You've never been.'

I knew she'd never been because I hadn't. I was amazed she'd even heard of the place. I mean we live in Leeds so we'd had a few day trips to the East Coast. Hornsea, Bridlington, Filey. But we'd never been to Scarborough. I was sure.

'Yes I have,' said Ally. 'I used to live there.'

Mum looked at Dad. Dad looked at Mum.

Here we go again, I thought. Was this another one of Ally's stories of a past life? One of her 'other family' fantasies? We were soon to find out.

Chapter 4

Dad said Disneyland would be a bit too expensive. He thought Greece would be too hot for me and Ally with us both being so fair and pale skinned.

Excuses, I was sure. Ally was going on and on about Scarborough. Wouldn't let it drop. I knew she'd get her way. I knew Dad would give in to her. He always does.

'It'll be great,' I heard him telling Mum later.

'The kids'll love the beach. And you really can't beat a good, old-fashioned British holiday.'

So at the start of the summer holidays, just before Ally's sixth birthday, we set off for a fortnight's holiday in Scarborough. Not exactly Disneyland and I can't say I was looking forward to it but I'd never seen Ally so happy. So excited. And, for the first few days of the holiday that's how it stayed.

OK, so it was a bit freaky when Ally kept shouting out:

'I remember that! I remember that shop!'

Or,

'That café wasn't there before.'

Mum and Dad kept looking at each other nervously. But Ally didn't seem to think it was at all weird that she claimed to know places in a strange town.

Funnily enough, she didn't have any nightmares while we were in Scarborough either. Mum said it was all the exercise and fresh sea air tiring Ally out. Dad said he didn't care what it was. He was just glad of a full night's sleep.

We were staying in a holiday cottage and, by the end of the first week we'd begun to run out of food, so Mum decided we were going to spend Friday morning in the supermarket. I moaned. Mum got cross. Everyone ended up shouting. So, of course the shopping trip was a bit of a disaster. But that was nothing compared to what happened on the way back!

We got a bit lost. Ended up driving round and round the streets, with Mum and Dad hot and flustered, snapping and snarling. Blaming each other.

'That's it!' Ally suddenly shouted out. 'That's my house! Where I used to live.'

Mum carried on driving. Ally started to scream. Louder and louder. Mum stopped the car.

'Don't be silly, Ally,' Mum said. 'You've never lived in Scarborough.'

'Yes, I have!' screamed Ally. 'With my other mummy and daddy. When I was a little girl. When I was Alison. Alison Smith.'

'OK,' said Dad. 'This is our chance. Why don't we put a stop to this once and for all?'

'What do you mean?' said Mum.

'Drive back,' said Dad. 'Knock on the door. Find out if anyone called Smith lives there.'

'Don't be ridiculous!' said Mum, turning all sort of purple. 'I'm not knocking on a stranger's door! I mean, what on earth would we say?'

'I'm not sure,' said Dad. 'I'll think of something.'

Mum stared at him as if he'd gone completely mad. Ally carried on sobbing.

'It might help,' Dad whispered. 'If we can prove to her how silly it all is...'

But what if it wasn't silly, I thought, as Mum reluctantly swung the car round. What if the people who lived there really were called Smith? What then?

I was actually shaking when Dad pressed the doorbell. I mean, part of me was sure it was all nonsense but it was sort of spooky all the same. The house even looked a bit spooky. It was an old, narrow terrace with ivy creeping round the porch.

For a while no one answered. We were just about to turn away when we heard sounds. Sounds of footsteps coming down the stairs. Then the door opened.

It was an Asian lady. I was so relieved! There were loads of Asian kids at my school and none of them was called Smith! It just isn't an Asian name. Or was I jumping to conclusions? There was nothing to say she wasn't married to a guy called Smith, was there?

As it happened, she wasn't. She was already shaking her head.

'Smith,' she said. 'No I don't think so. I don't know anyone round here called Smith.'

Great, I thought. Let's go.

'And have you lived here long?' Dad asked.

The lady looked at him suspiciously. Nervously. Who could blame her? With a family of strangers turning up, asking questions.

'About six years,' she said.

Then her face suddenly brightened.

'Now wait a minute,' she said. 'The people we bought the house from were called Smithers. Mr and Mrs Smithers. Elderly couple. It couldn't be them you were looking for, could it?'

Smith. Smithers. Both common enough names. Similar but different. Enough of a coincidence to be a bit creepy.

'They didn't move far away,' said the lady. 'I got the feeling they didn't want to move at all. But Mrs Smithers wasn't too well and they'd decided a bungalow would be easier. I'm sure I've still got the forwarding address for them. Would you like me to get it for you?'

'No,' said Mum, anxious to get away. 'It's all right.'

'Funnily enough,' said the lady. 'They were very keen for us to have the forwarding address. They said at the time, there was a chance someone might come looking for them.'

'Er... did they say who?' said Dad.

'Their daughter,' said the woman.

The woman looked at Mum.

'You're not...'

'No,' said Mum. 'No I'm not. I'm not their daughter.'

She grabbed hold of me and Ally and more or less dragged us back to the car.

Dad stayed for a minute or two longer. I saw him take a pen and a scrap of paper out of his jacket pocket. And I knew what he was doing. He was copying down that forwarding address.

I heard him and Mum arguing about it more than once during that second week of the holiday. Mum saying it was all stupid coincidence and no way were they going to check out the Smithers.

Ally kept pestering. Saying she wanted to go and see them. So I knew exactly what would happen on the Wednesday morning when Mum decided to go and have her hair cut.

Chapter 5

Dad was supposed to take us to the beach. But we took a little detour, didn't we? Ally was really excited. Dad looked a bit nervous. A bit guilty even. And me? I was just plain scared. Scared of what we might find.

We turned into an avenue full of bungalows and parked the car near the end of the street. Dad said we'd have a walk up. Just to see.

He took the scrap of paper out of his pocket.

Checked the address. All the time walking slowly. Outside one of the bungalows he paused. There was an elderly lady sitting outside in a wheelchair. Her head was down, reading a magazine. I think Dad was going to walk on but suddenly Ally let go of his hand and darted towards the gate.

She leant over, staring at the woman until the woman looked up.

'What's happened to you?' Ally cried out. 'What's happened to your legs?'

'Don't be so rude!' said Dad, grabbing Ally's hand.

'It's all right,' said the woman. 'Kids eh? Just blurt things out, don't they? It's not my legs, pet. It's my hips. Both of them falling to pieces, they are. I'm waiting to have an operation.'

'And your hair,' said Ally. 'It's grey. You look so old!'

The woman smiled but I could tell she was a bit offended.

'You don't know me,' said Ally, sadly.

'No I don't, sweetheart,' said the woman. 'What's your name?'

Dad had started to pull Ally away.

'I'm Alison,' said my sister. 'I'm Alison! You don't remember me! You don't remember. You were my...'

The woman let out a sharp cry, as Dad clamped his hand over Ally's mouth. At the same time an elderly man appeared in the open doorway.

'What is it, Barbara?' he said. 'What's wrong?'

'Who are you?' the woman said, staring at Dad. 'Why are you doing this? Leave me alone, can't you? Leave me alone.'

She began to turn her wheelchair round.

'What's happened?' said the man. 'What's going on?'

'She says she's Alison,' said the woman, pointing at my sister before propelling herself inside.

'I'm sorry,' said the man, coming towards us. 'My wife... well, she gets upset easily... if anything reminds her of... if she hears that name. We had a daughter called Alison too, you see.'

A flush spread across Ally's face while Dad and I turned pale. Dad had moved his hand from Ally's mouth but pulled her close to him to keep her quiet.

'Not that your little girl looks anything like our Alison,' said the man, as if to himself. 'And it's been a long time now. Over twenty years. But you never really get over something like that.'

'What happened?' said Dad, quietly.

He hadn't meant to ask. I knew he hadn't meant to. He just couldn't help himself. It was all just too weird.

'My Alison was a lovely girl,' said the man, his eyes misting over with memories. 'Never gave us any trouble, even as a teenager. She went to college, passed all her exams...we were ever so proud of her.'

He paused. Looked at us.

'Then, when she was just twenty-two years old, she disappeared,' he said. 'She'd been working as a nursery nurse at the local school but said she fancied a bit of a change. So she got a job as a nanny, for this rich family, who promised her all sorts of exciting trips abroad. But she never got to go anywhere. She'd only been with the family a couple of months when she disappeared. Alison just disappeared. The family said she robbed them. Left the children all alone one night and took off with the jewellery and ...'

'She didn't,' Ally suddenly shouted out. 'She didn't. That isn't true.'

'No, it wasn't true, pet,' said the man. 'My Alison could never have done anything like that. Something happened to her. Something terrible. She didn't steal anything. No matter what those people said.'

'Which people?' said Dad. 'Who was she working for?'

The man's face suddenly changed. Hardened.

'Who are you?' he said. 'Why are you asking all these questions? You're not a cop, are you? Or a journalist?'

'No,' said Dad.

'We used to get all sorts of cranks hanging round, asking questions,' the man said. 'But it was a long time ago. If you want to know anything else, it was all in the papers. Look it up.'

With that he turned, went inside and slammed the door, leaving me and Dad gawping, dazed and confused while Ally burst into tears.

'Don't tell your mother,' Dad pleaded on the way back. 'Not a word of this to Mum, do you understand?'

I knew he was scared Ally would blurt it out. But she didn't. In fact she was very quiet for the rest of the holiday.

If anything it was Dad who was edgy and acting strange. On the Friday before we went home he went to fill the car up with petrol and was gone for over two hours.

Mum reckoned he'd sneaked off to the bookies. Mum hates gambling but Dad likes a bet on the horses every now and again, when he thinks Mum won't find out. I thought he might have gone back to the Smithers but, naturally, I kept my thoughts to myself.

Mum and I were both wrong as it turned out but we didn't find out where Dad had really got to that day until almost two years later.

Strangely enough, during those next two years Ally was almost normal. It was like that visit to the Smithers had got something out of her system. She stopped saying weird things. Stopped talking about her 'other family', completely. Mum thought she'd just grown out of it all, like the doctors said she would.

Ally still had nightmares, sometimes. More than most kids, I'd say. But certainly not every night. Maybe no more than once every few weeks. And if Dad ever thought about what had happened in Scarborough, he didn't let on. We never talked about it.

I thought about it quite a lot, at first. Could it all have been coincidence? Possible. But the names...the fact that their daughter, Alison Smithers, had disappeared in mysterious circumstances. Creepy.

Maybe it was because it spooked me a bit, that I forced myself to stop thinking about it eventually. Or maybe my life just filled up with other things. School, mates, football. Everyday things.

The only time it came back to me was when

we did the Hindu religion in RE. Hindus believe in reincarnation. They think life's one big circle. You live, you die, you live again. Sometimes as a human. Sometimes not.

Some of my class thought it was all a bit of a laugh.

'Reckon you'll come back as a worm, next time,' they told each other. 'Or a slug. A squidgy, slimy slug.'

But I've got a couple of mates who are Hindu and they seem to accept it as perfectly normal. Not scary or spooky at all. And certainly not funny. I wanted to tell them about Ally but I was scared one of them might blab and it would be all over the school. Might even get back to my sister. And I didn't want that. Not when she seemed to have forgotten all about it.

Had she forgotten? I don't know. Obviously not completely because of what she did about twelve months ago.

Chapter 6

Ally was eight and I was in my last year at juniors. Years 3 and 4, which included Ally's class, went on a school trip to the Castle Museum in York. It was only a day trip. They set off, on a coach, at nine o'clock one Friday morning and were due back by four.

Even when the headmistress came to get me out of class just before lunch I didn't think it had anything to do with Ally. Why should I? The head looked a bit grim but then she always does. She's got a face like a rhino's bottom, at the best of times.

Like I said, I'm not particularly bright but I always try my best and I'm never in trouble at school. So I guessed the head just wanted me to do a job or something until I saw Mum and Dad standing outside the head's office. Mum was crying.

'Grab your coat, Tom,' Dad said, his voice tight and hoarse. 'We're going to York.'

'Ally!' I said. 'She's had an accident, hasn't she? What's happened? Tell me what's happened!'

I mean I know my sister's odd but she's still my sister and I love her to bits. So all sorts of terrible things raced through my mind. Road accidents. A fall. Or maybe she'd just been sick or something. Couldn't face coming home by coach.

'They've lost her,' Dad said, his voice angry now. 'They were looking round the museum, in groups. Ally was in a group with two teachers. Two of them and they couldn't watch a dozen kids properly!'

'It's a big place,' I said, remembering my own school trip there. 'It's easy to get lost. She'll be in there somewhere. I'm sure she will.'

'But she's been gone nearly two hours now,' Mum suddenly shrieked.

'They'll find her,' said Dad. 'Like Tom says. They'll find her.'

I don't think either of us felt as confident as we sounded. The drive seemed to take forever. Mum was crying down the phone to the teachers every couple of minutes. The answer was always the same. No news.

We were just driving into York, heading for the museum, when the phone rang.

'Oh thank goodness!' Mum screamed into it. 'Oh thank goodness! The police found her? Where? She's at the police station now. OK. Which way...right...yes...I've got it.'

She relayed the directions to Dad.

'She wasn't in the museum,' Mum said. 'They found her a mile or so away. Outside a house. Just standing there, on her own, staring at it.'

'I should have known,' said Dad. 'I should have known where she'd be.'

Mum and I both looked at him, mystified. Then he started to explain. Going back to that time in Scarborough when we went to see the Smithers.

'You went to see them!' Mum shrieked. 'And you never told me? None of you ever bothered to mention it to me?'

She ranted on and on. And all the time I was thinking... well, OK but what's the visit to the Smithers in Scarborough got to do with Ally going walkabout in York?

We'd stopped at some traffic lights when Mum finally stopped ranting and raving and Dad got a chance to explain.

'It all seemed too much to be coincidence,' said Dad. 'So that last day in Scarborough, when I went to fill the car up, I popped into the local library. Copied some old newspaper articles about the Alison Smithers case. I found out, amongst other things, that she was working for a family in YORK, when she disappeared.'

'And you told Ally!' Mum said.

'No,' said Dad. 'I didn't. I swear I didn't tell anyone. I tried to push it to the back of my mind.

Hid the copied articles amongst some old work stuff and tried to forget about it. I mean I did forget ... till a few minutes ago.'

There was a sudden blare of car horns. The traffic lights had changed. The people behind us were getting impatient.

Dad set off and minutes later we were at the police station. Mum and Dad hugged and kissed Ally. Everyone was talking at once.

I thought that would be it. We'd just take Ally home. But no. Once all the hugging, kissing and shrieking were over, a policeman showed us into an office and introduced us to a man called Walsh. A Detective Chief something or other. I didn't catch all of it but he sounded pretty important. Looked important too. Smart suit. Greyish hair. Serious, brooding sort of face.

Obviously a very senior cop so why was he involved in a case like this? Little girl wandering off on her own and found within two hours? I mean there was no one else involved. She hadn't been abducted or anything. She was safe. There was no real case. It didn't make sense.

'I don't quite know how to put this,' Walsh said, 'but your little girl has been telling my officers some very strange things.'

'Er, like what?' said Dad.

'Have you ever lived in York?' Walsh asked, seeming to ignore Dad's question. 'Or do you have any friends or family here, perhaps?'

Dad shook his head.

'Only the street where we found your daughter,' said Walsh. 'And the house she was standing outside, were once the scene of a rather unusual ... and unsolved ... robbery and missing person case.'

We knew who the missing person was, of course, before he told us. But we all kept quiet.

'It was a long time ago,' said Walsh. 'We probably wouldn't have even made the connection at all. Only it was your daughter who started talking about it. She knew about the theft. Even knew the name of the nanny who went missing. How would an eight-year-old who isn't even from the city know that?'

Good question, I thought. She could have pieced the story together from what Mr

Smithers said that day in Scarborough but how had she known which house it was? He hadn't even mentioned York! I was sure he hadn't. Could Dad have told Ally about it and then forgotten? Could she have found and read those articles he copied? She's dead nosy is Ally. Always rummaging about. So it was possible.

'I've told you,' Ally suddenly said. 'I know what happened because I lived there. I worked there. That was me!'

There was no way to avoid it. Not after everything Ally had said. So Mum and Dad told the detective everything. Right from the beginning. And he looked more than a touch bemused, as you can probably imagine.

'Whenever we have a major crime,' he said, at the end of our story, 'we have nutters phoning up claiming to be psychic. They tell us they know where the body is because they've seen it in a dream, or in a crystal ball or in the stars or something. Sometimes, if we're desperate, we follow it up. They're never, ever right!'

Well, that was it then. He didn't believe our

story. He thought we were loonies. And who could blame him?

'But this,' he said, 'this is different from anything I've ever come across before. Your daughter seems to know so much. Things she couldn't possibly know. We didn't ask her anything. We didn't question her. She just told us things!'

'Er... what sort of things?' said Dad, nervously.

Chapter 7

'Let me tell you a bit about the case first,' said Walsh. 'Alison Smithers was employed by a wealthy young couple to look after their three small children, Henry, Katherine and Marcus.'

Harry, Katy and Mark! The names Ally always uses when she plays! Like Smith and Smithers. Different but similar enough to make you shiver!

'Alison lived in, with the family,' Walsh went

on. 'The children's parents, Diane and Oliver Graystock, were pleased with her. She was very good with the kids. Seemed to absolutely adore them. Anyway, after Alison had been with the family for a couple of months, the parents went away for a weekend on business. They left on the Friday afternoon.'

All the time he was talking Ally was nodding and frowning at the same time. A deep crease appearing on her forehead like she was really concentrating. Trying to remember.

'When the couple came back, on the Sunday afternoon,' said Walsh. 'They noticed that some drawers and cupboards were open. Stuff had been thrown out onto the floor. They didn't even bother to check what was missing at first. They just rushed upstairs to look for their children.'

'Did they find them?' said Ally, clearly upset. 'Did they find the children? Were they all right?'

'Yes,' said Walsh. 'They found the children locked in their bedroom. Very distressed and frightened, of course, but otherwise unharmed.'

'Are you sure?' said Ally. 'Are you sure they were all right?'

'Yes, I'm sure,' said the detective. 'They were all very young... Marcus was just a baby, like you told me, Ally! So it didn't take the children long to get over their ordeal. But when the couple checked the house, they realised there were valuables missing. Money, jewellery, bank cards. A lot of paintings and works of art. The couple were art dealers, you see. Had a lot of stuff in the house. And, of course, the nanny was missing so...'

'They blamed her,' said Dad. 'Reckoned she'd robbed them, locked up the children and taken off.'

'It wasn't like that,' Ally shouted out. 'I've told you. It wasn't like that. I know!'

'I must say, it seemed odd, at the time,' said the detective. 'I wasn't in charge of the case but I worked on it. And I ran a full check on Alison Smithers. She'd never been in any trouble before. Not even at school. Wasn't involved in drugs, as far as we know. Didn't have a boyfriend, or seem to be involved with anyone with a criminal background. Wasn't paid very much but she wasn't in debt and didn't seem to have any money problems. Just didn't seem the type to do something like that really.'

'She didn't!' said Ally. 'Why won't you listen to me? She didn't do it! He killed her! He killed her!'

'Who killed her?' asked Dad picking Ally up as she started to cry. 'Who killed her?'

'I don't know,' sobbed Ally. 'I don't know. I can't remember. The man. The bad man.'

'Alison Smithers' parents always claimed she'd been murdered,' said Walsh. 'The longer time went on, the more certain they became. They were sure that if she'd still been alive, she would have been in touch. They were very close, apparently.'

Poor Ally was getting really upset at that point, so Mum took her off Dad and took her outside.

'We covered everything,' said the detective. 'Took that house apart. Nothing. Not a drop of blood. Not a single strange fingerprint. Not anything to hint there'd been a break-in, let alone a murder.'

'And the family,' said Dad. 'The family

Alison Smithers worked for. Do they still live there? In that house?'

'No,' said Walsh. 'They moved on long ago. The house has been turned into flats now. Rented out. To students mainly. But it was all a bit odd because ...'

He paused, as if wondering whether to tell us something. He obviously decided against it.

'I don't know,' he said. 'There were so many strange things about that case. I've got my own ideas about what might have happened. I've looked at the case time and time again over the years ... but without any forensic evidence and without the body ever turning up ...'

'Body?' I said. 'So you agree with Alison Smithers' parents? You think she WAS murdered.'

The detective smiled at me. But it was a sad sort of smile.

'It doesn't really matter what I think,' he said. 'I've never been able to prove anything and I doubt I ever will now. I'm due to retire in six months. But it bugs me to think there might be a killer out there who got away with it.'

'Maybe Ally could help,' I said.

Walsh smiled his sad smile again.

'Like I said, I've never ever believed in all this psychic nonsense and, convincing as your sister is, I don't really believe in it now. So I'm not prepared to upset her by further questioning. I mean, even if she claimed to remember something . . . something important . . . it's hardly evidence, is it? There's not a jury in the land who'd believe an eight-year-old girl who claimed to be a reincarnation of a murder victim, now is there?'

He was right, of course. Put like that, it sounded completely crazy. And even if Ally's memories were true, she still hadn't told them anything useful, had she? The best she'd ever been able to manage was that it was 'a bad man' who killed Alison Smithers. I mean murderers are hardly likely to be saints, now are they?

Ally was, understandably, tearful on the way home. Mum sat in the back of the car with her. Trying to comfort her. But telling her, too, that she mustn't ever wander off like that again. Not for any reason.

With all the upset and everything we knew there was no chance of Ally sleeping well that night but even so, we were terrified when we heard the scream.

Chapter 8

The screaming started around two o'clock and we all rushed into Ally's room. She was standing, pressed against the bedroom wall, her eyes wide open. Awake, yet not awake. Like she was in some sort of trance.

'Footsteps,' she said. 'There's someone downstairs. Moving about.'

We all knew she wasn't talking about our house. She was somewhere else. In some other time. Being someone else. A twenty-two-year-old nanny called Alison Smithers!

She lifted her right hand, making a twisting action with her wrist, like she was locking something. The children's door perhaps? Locking them in? Trying to protect them from whoever was downstairs?

Ally moved forward, while we all stood there, wondering what to do. Should we wake her? Touch her? Speak to her?

Before anyone could do anything her facial expression changed twice in quick succession. The trance-like blankness suddenly gave way to a smile and just as quickly gave way to a look of sheer terror and a scream so piercing that I grabbed hold of Dad, burying myself against him.

When I looked again, Ally was lying on the floor, Mum crouched beside her, holding her.

'I remember,' said Ally. 'I remember. I saw it all.'

She was sobbing and her eyes were still wide open, fixed and staring but she was clearly awake now. Mum lifted her, put her back in bed, sat stroking her hair.

'It's all right, sweetheart,' Mum said. 'It was just a dream. Another nasty dream.'

'No,' screamed Ally. 'It was real. I was there. It was him! It was him!'

'Who, darling?' said Mum.

'Rich,' said Ally. 'It was Rich.'

'Who's Rich?' I hissed at Dad.

'I don't know,' he whispered back. 'I've no idea.'

He stopped because Ally was talking again. Not as herself, of course, but as Alison Smithers.

'I heard the footsteps,' she said. 'I thought someone had broken in. I thought they might hurt the children. So I locked their door. I didn't know what to do. I wasn't sure. I crept downstairs. I was going to try to use the phone. Sneak out. Get help from a neighbour. I don't know. I'm not sure.'

'It was only a dream,' Mum started to say.

'No,' shrieked Ally again. 'Why don't you believe me? I remember. I remember. I was there! I got to the bottom of the stairs. The lounge door was open. One of the lamps was on ... very low. I saw him. It was Rich. It was only Rich.'

'And who was Rich?' Dad asked, quietly.

'Their dad,' said Ally. 'The children's daddy. It was only Rich. He'd come home.'

Well, Ally had been slightly wrong about names before. But I distinctly remembered the detective saying the children's parents were called Diane and Oliver. I mean Rich's short for Richard not Oliver. No way were they even similar!

'I went in,' said Ally. 'I saw what he was doing! He was taking things. Packing them into bags!'

Why? I thought, staring at my sister.

She seemed so wrapped up in it all. So convinced. As if she was really seeing it all. But if she was right, if it was the children's father, why was he robbing his own house? It didn't make sense. None of it made sense. Mum was right. This was only a dream. Not memories at all.

'There was someone else,' said Ally. 'Someone else in the room. A woman...she looked at me. I looked at her.'

'Who was it?' said Dad.

'I don't know,' said Ally, her voice rising to a really ear-piercing scream. 'I don't know! She said something. Rich turned round. He saw me! He looked scared. He came towards me. I didn't know. I didn't know what he was going to do! He put his hands on my shoulders. I didn't know! I still didn't know! His hands slid up to my neck . . .'

'That's enough! That's enough,' said Mum, clutching Ally close, hugging her fiercely. 'It's all right. It never happened, Ally. There was no bad man. No woman. Only a dream, darling. Only a nasty dream.'

I guess none of us got much sleep that night. I reckon I didn't doze off again till about seven a.m., so, of course, I slept in and, as it was Saturday, nobody bothered to wake me. When I finally crawled downstairs at about midday, Mum shoved a bowl of cereal in front of me and told me to hurry up, eat and get dressed. We were expecting a visitor.

I wasn't surprised to find that Dad had phoned that detective, Walsh. I knew Dad really believed all Ally's ramblings. But I was amazed that Walsh had decided to drive all the way to Leeds, on a Saturday, to see us, just because Ally had dreamt something again.

Two things had brought him rushing over, Walsh explained, when he arrived. One was the name Ally had used. Rich. Rich was Oliver's nickname from schooldays. It had come about when the teacher was asking them all one day what they wanted to be when they grew up. Most kids said the usual stuff. Teachers, footballers, models, vets. But when it had come to Oliver's turn he'd said:

'Rich. I want to be rich.'

As he was always wheeling and dealing, buying and selling, even as a kid, the name seemed to suit him and it stuck. Business colleagues knew him as Oliver or Mr Graystock but, at home, amongst family and friends, he was still Rich. Only someone who was close to him would know that!

Definitely creepy. Even Mum was spooked! But I was still wondering why Walsh was showing such interest. You could hardly arrest someone on the strength of a kid's dream, could you?

'I always had my suspicions about Oliver,' Walsh said.

'Why?' I said, unable to resist butting in. 'I mean he lived up to his nickname, didn't he? He became rich. So why would someone like that try to rob themselves?'

'Some people,' said Walsh, 'are never rich enough. They always want more. And some of them will go to any lengths to get it. Oliver got a massive insurance payout after the robbery. And, of course, if he'd stolen the stuff himself, he'd have eventually sold it off and gained twice over, wouldn't he?'

'But didn't you say he was away, at the time?' Mum asked. 'On a business trip? Surely he'd have had an alibi?'

'Ah,' said Walsh. 'That was another oddity. He and his wife, Diane, had gone to Manchester for a series of meetings and an art exhibition. Diane's parents live in Manchester, so, naturally enough, she chose to stay with them. But Oliver didn't. There'd been a few family problems, which I'll tell you about in a minute. Oliver had quarrelled with Diane's

56

father, so he chose to stay in a hotel. On his own . . . '

'So he could have driven back to York late on Saturday night,' Dad said. 'Committed the crime in the early hours of Sunday morning and still have been back in his hotel in time for breakfast!'

'He could,' said Walsh. 'Only his wife had the car. And we could never find any evidence that he'd hired a vehicle or anything like that. If he did do it, then he was very clever. Covered all his tracks.'

Once again, we seemed to be at a bit of a dead end. And I wondered why Walsh had bothered coming at all.

'The other thing that interested me about Ally's dream,' said Walsh, 'was the mention of another person in the room. A woman. You see that was what the family quarrel was about. A few weeks before the robbery, Diane's father had seen Oliver out with another woman. Accused him of having an affair. Oliver denied it all at the time and his wife, Diane, refused point-blank to believe it. All through the investigation Oliver gave the impression of being a perfect husband and father. There was no real evidence to link him to anyone else. But, then, about eighteen months after the robbery, Oliver left his family. Went off with someone called Nina. He's still with her.'

'Those sort of things happen,' said Mum. 'Families split up. It's sad, especially with three young children involved. But it doesn't make Ally's dream true and it doesn't mean the man's a murderer, does it?'

'No,' said Walsh, thoughtfully. 'But if he was planning to leave his family all along, it gives him more reason to want the insurance money, doesn't it? More reason to commit the robbery. And if Alison Smithers surprised him, as I always believed she did ... Saw his lady friend with him ... '

Ally would have chipped in, at that point, if she'd been there. But she wasn't. Mum had packed her off to a friend's for a couple of hours. She didn't want Ally getting all worked up again. So I guessed it was up to me.

'Even if it's all true,' I said. 'Even if he did

kill Alison Smithers, you can't prove it, can you? Not after twenty years!'

I liked Walsh. He always answered my questions. Never treated me like a kid or, even worse, an idiot. And he was always really nice to Ally too.

'I think I might have an idea,' he said. 'It's a bit of a risk. Not exactly in the rule book, if you know what I mean. Never thought it was worth trying before but if your sister was right... if there really was a woman with him that night... and if that woman was Nina... my idea might work. I'll need to check quite a lot of things first, though. Get special permission.'

He didn't say exactly what kind of 'special' permission or what his checks would involve but they certainly included questioning us for hours on end! Prying into absolutely everything.

I knew what he was trying to do. He was trying to find out whether we were genuine. Whether our stories, or rather Ally's stories, were for real. Whether we could have any secret connections with the Smithers or the Graystocks that we hadn't told him about. Or whether we were just a bunch of loonies!

Over the next few weeks, while he was gathering his information, Ally had a few more nightmares but they were back to being more normal. She didn't really remember anything when she woke. Just the feelings of anxiety which had plagued her all her life.

Me and Dad thought that the only way she'd ever be rid of them, the only chance she had of really being able to settle, was if Walsh finally solved the case. Which is why we went along with him, answering his endless questions.

Even Mum co-operated though I know she thought Walsh was mad. She thought we were all mad for believing, or even half believing, in Ally's dreams. She still does. Even after what happened.

Chapter 9

Not that anything seemed to be happening for a while. Not for weeks and weeks. I began to think Walsh might have changed his mind. Decided to just let it drop. After all, the murder, if that's what it turned out to be, had happened over twenty years ago.

Then, one night, just as I'd decided it had all fizzled out, Walsh turned up again. It was quite late. I'd just gone to bed but luckily, I wasn't asleep. I say luckily, because I was able to creep out and listen from halfway down the stairs!

'I've set something up,' said Walsh. 'If anything's going to happen it'll be in the next day or two.'

What had he done? I couldn't wait to hear. But unfortunately Mum was rattling around with teapots and cups and it was a few minutes before the noise settled.

'It's been done before,' Walsh said. 'Quite successfully in some cases.'

What had been done? What was he up to? Before I could decide whether to just burst in and ask, he was talking again.

'I've been given the go-ahead but it's still a bit of a risk,' Walsh said. 'If anything goes wrong, the newspapers'll be onto it in a flash... screaming police victimisation and all that rot... but what the heck! I'm retiring soon. What can they do to me? And if it works, well I'll be able to retire happily, won't I? Knowing I've finally got the...'

He said a bit of a of rude word, there. But it wasn't the word that shocked me so much as the fact that he was obviously bending, if not actually breaking, the rules. I mean, you don't really expect that of cops, do you? Even if it IS in a good cause! And I just hoped he knew what he was doing. As I said, I liked Walsh. I didn't want him to get into any trouble.

'They did something similar quite recently,' he was explaining. 'In a case down south. Bloke who'd murdered his wife. No proof, so they set up this sort of trap. Got the bloke, that time. But it doesn't always work so we only ever do it as a last resort.'

'What?' I wanted to shout out. 'What are you going to do?'

'We've bugged Oliver's house,' Walsh said, as if answering my question. 'Tomorrow someone's going to phone him and say that we've got some new evidence. Which is true in a way.'

'So what good will that do?' Dad asked.

'We're hoping to shock him and Nina into say-ing something . . . getting a confession on tape.'

Was that it? His clever plan? His rule bending? It didn't sound very dramatic to me. I don't know what I'd expected. Something more exciting. Midnight raids. Car chases. Police helicopters. I don't know. Something more interesting than bugging machines, anyway! I mean, there wasn't a chance of it working, was there?

Amazingly it did! Well, the first part of the plan anyway.

I've only ever heard those tapes once but it's the sort of thing that sticks in your mind and I think I can remember roughly how the conversation went.

Nina: 'The police have been on the phone! They say they've got some new evidence. About what happened to Alison.'

Oliver: 'Evidence? After all these years! They can't have. What sort of evidence?'

Nina: 'I don't know. They wouldn't say, on the phone. They're coming to see you! Tomorrow.'

Oliver: 'So what? Let them. It doesn't matter, does it? I'll just stick to my story, like I've always done.'

Nina: 'But what if they've found her? What if they've found the body?'

Oliver: (laughing) 'Won't be much left of it now, will there? Not after being in the water for twenty years! Besides, if anyone had dredged any bones out of the river, we'd have seen it on the news, wouldn't we?'

Nina: 'Not if the police had asked them to keep it quiet for a couple of days...'

Oliver: 'Look, I've told you. It doesn't matter, does it? They couldn't pin it on me at the time and they won't do it now. The only thing that could have ever connected me to Alison's disappearance was your car. And that's long gone.'

Nina: (tearfully) 'I suppose so. It's just that I don't know how you can be so calm about it! I still wake up thinking about her sometimes and I didn't even know the girl. I only ever saw her that once, when you...'

Oliver: 'I never meant to do it. You know that, don't you, Nina? It all happened so quickly. I never meant to kill her. She gave me a fright, that's all. Creeping down, like that. Seeing you with me! I should have thought. I should have made some excuse. But I didn't. I panicked...'

So there it was! Walsh had got a full confession on tape. Enough to charge Oliver Graystock with the murder of Alison Smithers. Enough to bring the case to court. But was it enough to get a conviction? Would the jury find him guilty? Or would they decide that a taped confession wasn't exactly solid evidence?

I didn't know this before but it takes ages to get a case to court and so the trial only started a couple of weeks ago, more than a year after the arrest. You might have heard about it. It was on TV and in all the papers.

What you won't have heard about, of course, is my sister's part in it all. The cops didn't think talk of reincarnation would go down too well with the judge and jury! So the whole case was going to rest on the tape.

It wasn't looking good. Oliver was still denying it all. Saying the police had tricked him. That the tape had been tampered with. That it was a forgery! But fortunately for Walsh, perhaps, Nina broke down in court on the fifth day of the trial. Ended up telling them everything!

It was unbelievable really. How cold and nasty Oliver had been. It was bad enough murdering poor Alison Smithers. But then he'd left his own kids locked up overnight! Can you imagine that? Not to mention all the lies he'd told over the years since.

I have to say I felt a bit sorry for Nina. The way she broke down, in court, it was obvious that the murder had played on her conscience all those years. That she was genuinely sorry for her part in it.

But Oliver... well, he didn't seem sorry at all. Just angry that he'd finally been caught out! He got a pretty light sentence, in the end, considering what he'd done. Only eight years. Even so Oliver's going to appeal and Walsh reckons the sentence might be reduced even further.

Who knows? I can't say I really care about Oliver Graystock anymore.

What I do care about, of course, is Ally. She's been so much better since the arrest. Sleeps right through the night now. And the memories, if that's what they were, really do seem to be fading completely.

Mum still won't accept the reincarnation theory. She swears Ally's just got an over-active imagination. That she must have somehow known about the case. Maybe seen something about it on TV sometime. Maybe even mixed up several different cases in her head. Perhaps later read those articles Dad had tucked away. Even noticed the hint that Oliver was having an affair. Set her fiery little brain to work. Spat out all the information in a series of terrifying nightmares.

Well, I'd like to believe Mum's right. I tell myself over and over that it was all just a series of bizarre coincidences. That there's no such thing as reincarnation. That my sister's not really weird at all.

Still, I was a bit worried the other night. Just

after the trial ended. When Mr and Mrs Smithers gave a brief TV interview.

I was sure Ally would flip when they appeared on the screen but she didn't. She just lay there, on the settee, staring. Her face set in that little frown she has.

They both looked much better, much happier than they'd done that day when we saw them in Scarborough. Mrs Smithers was walking, with the aid of a stick, so I guessed she'd had her hip operation. But it was Mr Smithers who spoke.

'We always knew Alison had died that night,' he said. 'So the news didn't really come as a shock to us. We're just pleased that the truth has finally been uncovered and that Alison's name has been cleared. We feel at peace now and we know Alison does too.'

I looked, nervously, at my sister sprawled on the settee. I needn't have worried. She was drifting off to sleep. Her eyes were starting to close and there was a smile on her face. A really peaceful smile.

The Foxcroft Files

Sandra Glover

Is there anything worse than starting at a new
school where your dad's the headmaster? Pike soon
finds out when he's befriended by Ryan Foxcroft.
Loud and aggressive, Ryan lies about his past and
attracts trouble. Trouble is, this makes him a prime
suspect when the school is hit by acts of sabotage.
But is he really responsible? In his efforts to defend
Ryan, uncover the truth and make sure his dad's
school passes the next inspection, Pike finds himself
getting involved with some very nasty people and
unravelling secrets which were never meant to be
discovered.

ISBN 1842702793   £4.99

e-(t)mail

Sandra Glover

Jason gets an email from an alien – definitely a
prank call, he thinks, particularly as it asks for the
mating habits of earthlings! However it becomes
serious when the mystery sender starts hacking into
his computer and over-writing his science project.
His best mate Tariq denies all knowledge of it, and
even Lucy, the class computer-whiz, can't help. Then
he gets scary visits from men in white coats and all
three of them start to consider the chance that it
really IS an alien – but will even the astro-scientists
confirm what's happening?

'A highly readable, dialogue-driven story.' T.E.S.

ISBN 1842700952 £3.99